MEL G

split image

a story in poems

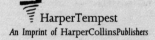

DISCARD

HarperTempest
An Imprint of HarperCollinsPublishers

Split Image
Copyright © 2000 by Mel Glenn

Library of Congress Cataloging-in-Publication Data
Glenn, Mel.
  Split image: a story in poems / Mel Glenn.
    p.   cm.
  Summary: A series of poems reflect the thoughts and feelings of
various people—students, the librarian, parents, the principal, and
others—about the seemingly perfect Laura Li and her life inside
and out of Tower High School.
  ISBN 0-688-16249-5 — ISBN 0-06-000481-9 (pbk.)
  1. High school students—United States—Poetry.   2. Suicide
victims—United States—Poetry.   3. Teenagers—Suicidal
behavior—Poetry.   4. Teenage girls—United States—Poetry.
5. Chinese American teenagers—Poetry.   6. Young adult poetry,
American.   [1. High schools—Poetry.   2. Chinese Americans—
Poetry.   3. Suicide—Poetry.   4. Schools—Poetry.   5. American
poetry.] I. Title. PS3557.L447 S65   2000   99-46041
811'.54—dc21   CIP
                                                                         AC

◆

First Harper Tempest edition, 2002

Visit us on the World Wide Web!
www.harperchildrens.com

For my mother, Liselotte

Prologue

Laura Li

Am I my brother's keeper?
Am I the one
Forced by my mother
To *be* the mother,
To care for and protect
My big brother, Jimmy,
From the ravages of his illness?
Am I my brother's keeper?
I love him every day;
I loathe him every day,
As I wash, dress, and feed him.
I can't tell you how many plans
Are crushed by what I must do for him.
I can't tell you how many friends
Are lost because I'm ashamed to invite
    them over.
I can't tell you how many colleges
Are pipe dreams because I must stay at home.
Jimmy is not responsible for who he is.
Am I?
If I am to be my brother's keeper,

What can keep me from
Rattling the bars of my own caged rage,
Never uttering a word back in anger?

Jimmy Li

Hold my hand, my sister,
Hold my hand.
Hold my heart, my sister,
Hold my heart.
Never let go of either.
The ocean is wide,
The boat is rocking,
And I am so scared and so alone.
When I was hiding,
You found me in the smoking room,
Emptying out ashtrays one by one on the floor.
You brought me up on deck
To taste the fresh air,
To show me the Great Wall of China at my back
And the Statue of Liberty in front of me.
Help me, sister, help me.
Where are you?
I cannot find your hand.
I feel myself slipping away softly
Under the dark blue cover of the sea.
Sister, sister, will you join me?
Will you come for me soon?

Laura Li

At night, when I was little,
When I had just come to America,
I'd pretend that we'd soon go back to China,
Just my father and me.
But now he is always flying
To this city or that continent,
And I hardly get a chance to see him.
I'd like to talk to him about serious things,
But now there is only time to say good-bye
        between departures.
My father always promises me that
He will take me on his next business trip.
But my mother always says I am needed at home.
My mother wins; my father leaves—
The typical flight pattern in our house.
My father is AWOL—
Absent without my leave.
Oh, Father, take my hand,
Take me out to the airport, please.
We'll get on a big plane and fly away—
Together.

Oi Pin Li

I talk to you, my daughter,
As I would to a small plant.
I watch as you grow taller with every season.
I water you with wisdom;
I clip your branches, should you grow too wild.
I provide a rich soil for you here in this new country.
This poor gardener asks but one thing:
When you grow to your full height,
You are to provide shade
For your older brother,
Whose own growth is stunted.
Because he will never grow on his own,
You must care for him as I care for you.
You must watch over him as I watch over you.
When I am gone, you are to be
More mother than sister to him.
I charge you with this responsibility,
For the roots of the family tree
Are never allowed to grow alone.
The roots of the family tree
Must always intertwine.

You are a wonderful little plant, my darling.
I see the sunlight in your eyes.

Laura Li

My grandmother's teakettle,
Made of fine china,
Sits on the high shelf,
Proper in its space,
Pristine in its beauty.
It is to be admired
From afar.
It is to be noticed
For its smooth, curved lines.
It is to be handled
Gently, delicately,
Only on special occasions.
Ah, little teakettle,
Poised on your high shelf,
Wait until you
Gather your own steam
And watch
As I boil over.

Charles Li

I have business interests around the world.

I am known in Kuala Lumpur.

I am honored in Hong Kong.

I am praised in Paris.

I am lauded in London.

I can tell you about the best hotels.

I can tell you about the best airports.

I can tell you about the best restaurants.

I can tell you about the best restaurants

In the best hotels in the best airports.

No, I can't tell you what grade my daughter is in.

Her mother would know that.

No, I can't tell you what clothes she wears.

Her mother would know that, too.

Yes, I have interests all over the world.

Yes, I have many important meetings to attend.

I don't take care of business at home.

Why don't you ask her mother?

Why do you ask me these questions?

PUBLIC
ADDRESS
ANNOUNCEMENT

The library is now open.

Guy Blankenship

The library?

I think it's on the third floor.

Why are you going up there, man?

Nobody reads anything anymore.

Book reports? Research papers? Get real.

You can get those things delivered to your house,

Like pizza.

Or you can pull them off the Internet.

Just in case, I got my one book.

It's a book I been usin' since the fifth grade.

It's about this dumb guy

Who finds a pearl

And people try to steal it off him.

Cool.

Oh, and at the end of the book?

This idiot throws it back into the ocean.

You still going up there?

Oh, you're meeting someone.

That's different.

Yeah, it's on the third floor,

Or the second.

I forget which.

Sarah Binder,
Librarian

That was then. . . .

> When I was a little girl,
> I would read for hours under the covers,
> Until I would fall asleep
> With my head resting on the pages
> And the flashlight still turned on.
> As I was growing up,
> The nights made me forget
> The days of junior-high terror
> And high-school anonymity.

This is now. . . .

> Now I run, not a library, but a media center.
> I have information on thousands of different
>   subjects,
> Or know where to get it.
> Every day I unlock the same wooden door
> And open new worlds for hundreds.
> I give book talks, attend conferences—
> I'm proud to be a librarian.

Oh, and I hire monitors. You interested?

What's your name again? Laura Li?
Why do you want to work here?
You like books?
Well, that serves as an introduction,
But it's not the whole story.

Lana Novakova
Yana Novakova

I hate the books in the library,
Nobody looks in the library,
Nothing but kooks in the library,
I loathe every nook in the library.
    I like to be in the library,
    Books are for free in the library,
    You can cut period three in the library,
    It's Laura I see in the library.
I've become a big bore in the library,
I'd rather snore in the library,
I'll scream, "No more!" in the library,
Show me the door in the library.
    I like to sit in the library,
    I love having writ in the library,
    I eat a bit in the library,
    I'm one who fits in the library.

Sarah Binder,
Librarian

Just tell people at a cocktail party you're a librarian
And watch how conversation ceases.
"Read any good books lately?" they ask politely,
And then go to find someone presumedly more
    interesting.
They dismiss me as quickly as they would turn a page.
Let them go; they don't know what they're missing.
I can discuss the arts of countries around the world.
I can argue about the politics of those countries, too.
I can swap risqué stories in three languages.
I'm so well-rounded I roll—I rock and roll.
But if those cocktail party people don't want to
    listen to me,
I always have my steadfast friends,
Like Huck and Jim, Romeo and Juliet, Heathcliff and
    Catherine.
So in the morning when I turn on the lights,
Put up the coffee, switch on the AC and the computers,
I say hello to those friends who have a long shelf life.
Now I am teaching Laura Li how to open up in the
    morning.

I have given her a spare key and a locker of her own.
She won't have long to wait
Before she hears my friends
Speaking to her across the centuries.

Sarah Binder,
Librarian

The daughter I had was bright and beautiful.
In the quiet language of mothers and daughters,
She learned at my knee,
And then, as she grew older,
At my elbow, and finally,
At my level, where, these days,
We don't see eye to eye very much anymore.
She's away at college now,
And grudgingly comes home for vacations,
When we replay the old arguments in taped loops,
Fighting about everything from
The color of her boyfriends
To the color of my nail polish.
I love her, but don't like her much as we both
Count down the time 'til she goes back to school.
We had too many battles,
To ever walk again along
The sweet green path of serenity.
I look now to Laura Li,
And realize that in my teaching her
What I know, what I do,

I am trying to repair the damage
I did to myself, I did to my daughter,
My daughter who is so bright and beautiful.

Laura Li

Ms. Binder treats me
Like I was her daughter.
If I sneeze, she says,
"Are you all right, dear?"
If I cough, she says,
"Do you want to see the school nurse?"
If I can't reach a high shelf, she says,
"Shall I get you a stepladder, Laura?"
Whenever I run an errand, file an article,
Restack the returned books, put out the magazines,
She thanks me as if I had performed
The most difficult task imaginable.
Whenever I learn something new about cataloging,
She marvels at how intelligent I am.
In her eyes, I can do no wrong.
I am the best worker she has ever had.
In my mother's eyes, I can do no right.
I am the worst worker she has ever known.
Can both these people really be me?
Ms. Binder is like a mother to me.
I wish my own mother were more
Like a mother to me.

Laura Li

What I say to my mother:
Yes, Mother, yes, Mother, yes.
I am a good child,
Even better than your first-born, Jimmy.
He is the child who is worthy enough
To receive all of your love,
The one who is gentle enough in your eyes
To receive the warmth of your arms.
Yes, Mother, I will do anything you ask,
To prove that a second-born
Can take first place in your heart.

What I don't say to my mother:
No, Mother, no, Mother, no.
I am an evil child,
Even worse than your first-born, Jimmy.
I am the child who is not worthy enough
To receive any portion of your love,
The one who is not gentle enough in your eyes
To receive any measure of affection from you.
No, Mother, I will not do anything you ask
To prove that a second-born
Can take first place in your heart.

Laura Li

Daddy, do you have to go?
I know your job is important,
That it takes you to places
I've never heard of.
But do you think people
In places I've never heard of
Love you half as much as I do?
Please take me with you.
I'll pack your bag.
I'll carry your bag.
I'll unpack your bag.
And when you're not working
At your important job,
You can take me to beautiful parks
In cities I have never heard of,
And afterward you can buy me coffee
At an outdoor café, where
We can watch the people passing by.
I can make you laugh by mimicking
The languages I have never heard before.
Daddy, do you have to go?

Laura Li

My brother sails the air currents,
Watching TV endlessly from morning to night.
He navigates the channels with his remote,
Logging in so many hours his finger sports a callus.
Program after continuous program
Washes over him like a sea of sound.
He scans the nighttime skies,
Pulling in show after show from all over the world.
Seated in his captain's chair in the living room,
A cigarette dangling from his mouth,
He issues direct orders from the bridge:
"Get me this, bring me that, and hurry, please."
Orders that I, the cabin girl, must perform.
Is it not bad enough that I am commissioned to
Cook for him, clean for him, do for him?
Is it not the ultimate embarrassment
That I must wash him, as well?
I wish to leave forever this sinking family ship,
But cannot, for reasons of duty, honor—and fear.
My mother still reigns as admiral of the seas—with lash—

While my brother still sails the Technicolor seas into
    oblivion.
Someday soon a mutiny will break out
And all hands will be lost.

Jimmy Li

Sister, sister,
Can you get me an orange?
One that is not too hard, not too soft,
If it's not too much trouble.
Sister, sister,
Can you get me a pillow?
One that is not too hard, not too soft,
If it's not too much trouble.
Sister, sister,
Can you adjust the light?
So that it is not too dark, nor too bright.
I'm afraid of the dark.
Sister, sister,
Can you adjust the heat?
So that it is not too hot, nor too cold.
I'm afraid of freezing.
I would do all this for myself, if I could.
And I wish I could do everything for you.
I love you so much; do you love me?
Of course you do, that's what you always say.
You always say, "I can't live without you."
Sister, sister, I'm hungry now.

Can you prepare my dinner?
If it's not too much trouble.

Laura Li

Hugs are not enough, my brother,
Especially those laced with my bitterness.
Even if my love were purely golden,
It could not fill the abyss of your pain or mine.
All your visits to doctors in different cities
Cannot locate the compass point of your cure.
All the medicines I give you
Only mask the weakening of your body.
I have modeled a life in school
To protect me against the flood of your illness.
But when I come home, the dam breaking,
With you sitting in front of the TV,
It serves as a constant reminder
That, save for a slight nudge in the cosmos,
I might be sitting in your chair,
On the other side of the dam.
It is then I realize that hugs,
Especially halfhearted ones,
Are not enough to make either you or me
Safe.

Alejandro Felix

The library?

Hey, man, you won't catch me up there.

It's for geeks and stuff.

So why am I going?

My mother found this overdue book

Under my mattress.

She freaked.

What's she getting a cardiac for?

It was only from last year.

So I'll just run up and run down.

You wanna wait? I'll only be a sec.

Oh, hello.

You work here?

Since when?

I come here all the time.

Never saw you, though.

I need some help with this research paper.

Can you help me?

Can I take you out?

Can I put a reserve on you?

What do you mean,
You "don't circulate."

Ernesto Rojas

Where you been, man?

We gotta get out to the track.

How come you took so long?

They givin' away books?

You don't read nothin' but the racing form anyways.

A girl? What girl?

You crazy, man?

You tryin' to make a librarian?

You puttin' your money on the wrong filly.

What do you mean, she's a Thoroughbred?

What did you do, man, check her teeth?

How much do you wanna bet

If she's that gorgeous

Someone else's riding her to the finish line?

How much you wanna bet

If she's the class of the field

You ain't gonna win, place, or show?

You comin' with me to the track, or what?

I ain't gonna wait for you

Furlong.

Alejandro Felix

Face it, Ms. B., you want to hire me
For the library squad. I'm your man.
I'm young, strong, and very good-looking.
You need books moved?
You need chairs picked up?
You need to keep the young ones in line?
I'll be better than anyone you can get.
What do I like about libraries?
Tell you the truth, Ms. B.,
It's not the books—it's the quiet.
The halls, the classrooms, the whole school,
They're so noisy, you can't hear yourself think.
Same thing as my house, everyone screaming at
    each other.
This is the one sane place in the entire building.
I got the job? You mean it?
I love you, Ms. B. I won't let you down.
I'll be working with Laura Li?
Who's that? The girl over there?
Is she new?
I've never seen her before.

Alejandro Felix

You stereotyping me?
Are you stereotyping me?
Hey, man, just because I speak Spanish,
Doesn't mean I work on a bean farm,
Doesn't mean I eat tortillas and burritos,
Doesn't mean I live at Taco Bell.
Actually, I work part-time in the library.
Actually, I love pastrami on rye.
Actually, I go to art museums—
Well, sometimes, at least.
I love some French wines,
A few German beers,
And a couple of Italian desserts.
I like Israeli oranges,
Japanese sushi,
And Swedish meatballs.
Also keep in mind,
I love women from all over
To be all over me.
So don't go stereotyping me,
And telling me to
"Stick to my own kind,"

Because my tastes transcend
All borders.

Shirley Eng

Though Laura Li is not my closest friend,
We do talk about the many things
We have in common,
Like doing chores,
Which we both hate.
When I get home from school,
I must do the shopping and the cleaning
Because my mother is working
And my father has more important things to do,
Like reading the afternoon newspaper.
When Laura Li comes home from school,
She must do the cleaning and the laundry
Because her father is working
And her mother has more important things to do,
Like working in a real estate office.
Laura Li hates doing the laundry.
"I am not a peasant," she says.
I laugh as she tells me
She loses her brother's socks on purpose
And sweeps the dust under her brother's bed.
Laura Li does not laugh at all and I quickly
Bring up another subject to talk about.

Victoria Hermosa

The old crones in my neighborhood
Squat on the stone steps of their apartment buildings
And peer up and down the block,
Noting with hawklike intensity
The slightest change
In the atmosphere.
A sly grimace here,
A darting look there
Sends the clarion call of something amiss,
Something outside the natural order
Of avian activities.
So when I brought my friend Laura Li home
To see my collection of seashells,
I must have ruffled quite a few feathers,
For the flock stopped in mid-cackle,
Their mouths agape, and waited until
The white dove with long black plumage and I passed by
So they could scratch the ground
For the seeds of their gossip
And spread them in ever-widening circles.

Arthur Feldman

"You will go to yeshiva, if God desires,
Not to public high school," my mother said.
"You will go to temple, if God desires,
Not play basketball on Saturdays," my mother
        said.
My mother can say anything she wants,
But I'm not going to listen to her, or God; it's
        my life.
I told her I was going to Tower High School,
That I wanted friends from all over.
And perhaps, just perhaps, there was no such being
        as God.
She leaned over the table
And smacked me hard across the face.
"He lives in this house—don't you forget that."
I ran into my room, slammed the door, and
Wondered if I could change religions.
Through the door I heard my mother
Crying on the phone to her sister,
"He had such a nice Bar Mitzvah."
This all happened four years ago.

I went to Tower; she got tired of fighting.

I will always be thirteen years old in her eyes.

Arthur Feldman
Alejandro Felix

"Hey, man, what you doin' in the library?"

    "I work here, remember. You?"

"Just chillin', couldn't hack math today."

    "Hey, where's the girl I seen you with?"

"I got put in the we're-good-friends category."

    "That's messed up."

"All girls suck. Didn't I see you hittin' on Laura Li?"

    "I was, but she shot me down.

    In a nice way, though."

"I hear she's a virgin."

    "I hear she's a nympho."

"I hear she's goin' away to school."

    "I hear she's going to drop out."

"You gonna try again?"

    "I'm thinking about it.

    The way she locks on to you

    With those eyes of hers?

    Man, she seems to know what you're

    Thinking and it's all right.

    You don't feel like an asshole

    Talking to her.

And she doesn't giggle like girls do."

"Maybe that's love."

"Yeah, maybe."

Love Letter #1

To say the sky is beautiful
Does not describe its many shadings.
To say the grass is green
Does not describe its brilliant color.
To find the words that will encompass my heart's longing
Lies beyond the scope of my well-worn thesaurus.
When I first saw you in the library that day,
Caressing a book as if it were a warm kitten,
I wished to be that book in your hands.
I found myself going to the library more often.
I found myself taking out books
On subjects I had no interest in,
Just to hear you say, "Next."
I want to be next to you.
I need to be in the library,
Surrounded by words, millions of words,
That would help me explain
How much I love you.

Love,

A.F.

PUBLIC ADDRESS ANNOUNCEMENT

All students and teachers
are urged to use the library
during their free periods.

Amy Yau

I do not know her father's name.
I have never seen her house.
I do not know her phone number.
I have never seen her mother.
When the library opens in the morning,
She's already there, smiling gently.
Sharp and crisp as a hostess,
She welcomes you to the sunlit porches
Of Tara and Campobello.
"How can I help you? What do you want to read?"
She whispers in a voice that gently
Washes over you, like a spring sun-shower.
I am her best friend, they tell me,
Measured by the number of classes we share.
But I am really not that close to her,
Measured by the distance she keeps from me.
I have never entered her father's house.
I do not even know his name.

LaToya Johnson

Who am I?
What is the road?
How to behave?
What is the code?
History paper,
Way past due,
Topic: world religions,
Don't have a clue.
If I am a Jew, who are you?
Druid, please, just a tease.
Dalai Lama, instant karma.
Go to mass, think I'll pass.
Methodist, makes my list.
Latter-Day Saints, think I cain't.
Follow the Koran, if I can.
Library, library,
Which one to take?
For my report, for my life,
Which one, for heaven's sake?
So many paths,
Difficult decisions.
Sitting in the library,
Losing my religion.

Thomas Moorehead

I should be writing my report on world religions,
Like LaToya is doing over at the next table.
But the world has no religion,
Or morality,
Or justice.
Look at the newspaper on the rack:
Page 1—Congressman Caught with His Pants Down
Page 2—Suicide Bomber Shatters Fourteen Lives
Page 3—Civil War Rages in West Africa
Page 4—Priest Mugged on City Street
Page 5—Newborn Baby Retrieved from Dumpster
Nobody says what the world should be.
They just say that's the way the world is.
I'd like to join:
1—The Peace Corps
2—The Salvation Army
3—The United Nations
4—Feed the Children
5—Greenpeace
I'd like to change the world right now.
But first I've got to finish
My history paper.

Eddie Sabinsky

If there were no more libraries,
Teachers couldn't give book reports.
If there were no more book reports,
Teachers would have less to read.
If teachers had less to read,
They would be more relaxed.
If they were more relaxed,
There would be more time to hang out.
If there were more time to hang out,
Students would feel less stressed.
If students felt less stressed,
They would have more time to read.
If they had more time to read,
There would have to be
Many more libraries.

Nothing much, Ms. B.,
Just hanging out,
Thinking about a few things.

Beatrice Scarpetta,
Teacher

Laura Li,

Did any new travel magazines come in?

I'd like to start planning my summer vacation.

What are you doing for the summer?

Oh, it's all right not to know.

What college are you going to?

Oh, it's all right not to be sure.

Do you want to be a librarian?

Oh, it's all right to keep your options open.

To tell you the truth,

I graduated with an English major.

That's a major for all those

Who aren't sure what their major should be.

And to think I've been at Tower over twenty years.

My mother? Thank you for asking.

As well as can be expected.

I visit her nearly every week.

She can be a little demanding, you know.

My summer plans?

I'd like to see Venice again.

This time without my mother.

Oh, you've found one? On Venice?
Aren't you a dear.

Diana Colón

Laura Li,

You got any books on the military?

Marines actually.

My father wants me to read about 'em.

He gives me no credit for anything.

I can't believe he'd like me to

Crawl on my stomach and eat lousy food.

For God?

For Country?

Naah, none of that.

He wants me to join the marines

So he don't have to pay no college tuition.

I swear, Parris Island ain't gonna be good for

My nails, my hair, my body.

I'm gonna get muscles where I don't even want 'em.

I don't wanna be part of

The few, the proud, the brave.

If I go to basic training,

I'm gonna be part of

The many, the broken, the ugly.

I gotta admit, their dress blues are kind of snappy,

But the regular uniform hardly makes a fashion statement.

Maybe the marines do want a few good women,
But I ain't gonna be one of 'em.
I'm goin' shopping,
With my father's credit card, of course.

Eddie Sabinsky

"The college guides are all
In the reference section, Eddie,"
Ms. Binder tells me as she points
To the back of the library,
Where the introductions to my future
Stand like arrogant soldiers
Ready to salute me in clipped cadences.
The 50 Best Colleges,
The 10 Best Buys,
20 State University Bargains.
How can one book tell me which college to choose?
How can one book tell me what to do with my life?
All these printed pages do nothing to relieve
The anxiety I feel in the pit of my stomach.
Does quoting the teacher/student ratio,
The size of fraternities,
The number of Nobel Prize–winners,
Lay out for me what I am to do with my life?
Ms. B., you gotta do better than this.
Do you have any books that will
Open my window to the world
And show me in glorious detail

The exact composition of the road
I am to travel?

Sarah Binder,
Librarian

"Old, old maid,
Hardly paid,"
They decry,
Such a lie.
Truth be told,
They're so old.
Done it all,
Walking tall.
Slept in Nome,
Ate in Rome.
Hiked in Maine,
Loved in Spain.
Saw Riyadh,
Also Chad.
Conference, Frisco
And San Luis Obispo.
Played in Rio,
Danced with brio.
QE II,
Timbuktu.
Toured Far East,

Met Kenya's beasts.
Standing proud,
I shout loud:
I've done so much, can't you see?
Admit it, then: You'd like to be me.

Library Fun

V
E
R
T
I
C
A
L

F
I
L
E

LARGE PRINT

BOOK . . . . ENDS

Laura Li

There's Harvard,
There's Yale,
There's everyplace else.
To dream of walking
Through fall leaves
At some prestigious Ivy League university,
To dream of attending
Special lectures
At some prestigious state university,
To dream of making new friends
At some prestigious liberal arts university.
I'm free to dream all I want.
North, south, east, west,
My mind can travel to any campus.
My body? Well, that's another story,
Because my mother has said
That I must stay home
To take care of "my responsibilities."
I may only apply locally,
To some prestigious institution in this city.
I may only apply
To the college of her choice.

Laura Li

USC,
Could be me.
LSU,
I could do.
U. of Penn,
Rates a ten.
Maybe Rice,
Would be nice.
Perhaps Yale,
In the mail.
U. of Minn,
I'd get in.
NC State,
That'd be great.
U. of Mass,
Freshman class.
In many words, my
Mother has spoken,
"You'll do as I wish."
My dreams lie broken.

Kiran Singh

Laura Li,
I am not a doctor,
Nor do I wish to become one,
But right now I must research
All the material you have on
Bypass operations.
For, you see, as we speak,
My father is having such an operation.
I wanted to go to the hospital
To be with him, but my mother said,
"The best medicine for you is to go to school."
I fear I cannot concentrate on my studies.
Oh, my father is so brave and so strong.
He has survived the monsoon and the dust.
He will survive this, I believe.
I will pray for his recovery.
Then this afternoon I will speed to his bedside
And wait while he gathers his strength again.
Oh, Father, do not worry, I will not leave you.
Soon I will be only a heartbeat away.

Jonathan Dampier,
Teacher

Incoming, incoming.

"Can I leave the room?"

"I don't have my homework."

"What homework?"

"I'm gonna be sick."

"It's too hot in here."

"It's too cold."

"I gotta see the nurse."

"I gotta see my guidance counselor."

"My mother just beeped me."

"I forgot my book."

"Which book?"

"The bus broke down."

"My car had a flat."

"I can't read your handwriting."

"What was the question?"

Shell-shocked,
I come here to the library
On my free period
For a little R and R

Before I have to
Return to the front lines
Of the Pubic Wars.

Clyde Dunston

My friend gave me this here reading list.
And my teacher says if I don't
Do this here book report,
I shouldn't make summer plans, 'cause
He's gonna fail me for sure.
You got any of these books, Ms. Binder?
Death by a Salesman,
Inherit the Breeze,
1983,
Catcher in the Wheat,
Lord of the Ties,
Raisin Eaten by the Son,
The Drapes of Roth,
Scarlet Litter,
To Kill a Vulture,
The Merchant of Tennis.
You got any of these, Ms. B.?
I really don't want to fail
And go to summer school.
Why are you laughing?

Josie George

My mother says I'll be late for everything:
My wedding,
My classes,
My job,
My funeral, probably.
"You were even born two weeks late," she says.
I can't help it if I'm always late.
My first-period teacher says to me,
"Howdy, stranger, new in these parts?"
He thinks he's funny.
I can't help it if I'm late to work.
My shift boss says to me,
"Do all the buses you take automatically break down?"
He thinks he's funny.
I am late to
Parties, checkups, dates,
Cheerleading practice, exams, and the orthodontist.
This is not funny:
Laura Li,
Do you have any books on pregnancy?

I think I may be
Late
Big time,
This time.

Tyesha Hicks

Laura Li, let me tell ya,
I used to live with my mom,
'Fore she moved away to Philadelphia.
I used to live with my grandma
'Fore she up and died on me.
I used to live with my best friend
'Fore her mom got tired of feedin' me.
I wanted to move in with my boyfriend,
But Child Welfare wasn't havin' none of that.
They placed me in a foster home,
Which I ran away from
'Cause the old man there tried to grab me.
Now I'm in another foster home,
Which ain't too bad
'Cause I eat regular and have my own room.
And the old man there leaves me alone.
He looks creepy, but hasn't tried anythin'—yet.
Someday I'm gonna have a place of my own
And not worry 'bout anyone messin' with me.
Living in a foster home
Sure don't foster
Any sense of home.

Eugene Gaffney, Jr.

Laura Li lets me
Sneak into the library
Because she knows
The crazies are all out there.
She tells me to sit in the corner,
Look busy,
And if she can find one,
Brings me a copy of
The latest in-line skating magazine.
The wheels are my passion, man.
"We'll go skating sometime," she whispers.
And the way she says it
Makes it sound better than
"We'll have sex sometime."
Laura Li knows that,
When I'm flyin' down the road,
I don't think about the teachers
Who hassle me in class.
I don't think about the guidance counselors
Who want to screw with my head.
I don't think about my father
Who calls me a "bum on wheels."

I think about skating with Laura Li
And try to forget about all those people
Telling me, day after day, to get
In line.

Robyn Jacobs

When I was eleven,
I picked up the extension
And heard my father
Talk mushy love words.
He wasn't talking to my mother.
I didn't speak to him for weeks.
When I was twelve,
My mother picked up the extension
And heard my father
Speak of weekend getaways.
He wasn't talking about plans with my mother.
She didn't speak to him for months.
My family trembled on the edge of divorce,
Until therapy patched together
The torn fabric of our lives.
Laura Li, you got any books on psychology here?
There are still some shreds to stitch together.
I think when I grow up
I might become a therapist
And treat myself even more.

Carl Snider

Laura Li,
You got any sports magazines?
It don't matter which ones—
Football, basketball, or baseball,
I read 'em all.
I like keeping the stats:
Rushing yards gained per game,
Foul shots scored per game,
Earned runs yielded per game.
I take all the numbers,
Drop them into my computer,
And can easily predict
Who's gonna win on any particular night.
I'd like to be a statistician
When I get outta high school,
That is, if I get outta high school.
I'm failing math—
For the fourth time.
I don't understand it either.
What are the odds on that?
You got the latest *Sports Illustrated*?
I'll bring it back to the front desk when I'm finished.

Tyesha Hicks

Hey, girlfriend, what's up with you?
Ain't seen you around lately.
How come you workin' that side of the desk?
Ain't they got teachers for that?
Lose the library, girlfriend, and
We'll go over to my house and chill.
Or maybe we'll pick up some guys,
A black one for you and an Asian one for me.
Mix and match, I always say.
What you mean, you can't?
These books ain't walkin' away.
They been here for centuries—
Ain't nobody wants to steal 'em.
Hey, now don't you be givin' me that princess pose.
You ain't no better than anyone else.
You just think you is.
But I like you anyways.
Hey, ditch this place, girl, and come out with me.
We'll have fun and do stuff.
What's fun?
It's somethin' you ain't havin' here right now,
Not that I can see anyways.

Eugene Gaffney, Sr.,
Parent

(telephone call)

Guidance Office?
Before you say a word,
Let me tell you a few things.
My boy has been in your school for two years
And I'm sure you don't know who he is.
I found his last report card under his bed.
He failed nearly everything.
Don't your teachers do anything?
Don't you call parents if someone is in trouble?
Or do you let them slip through the cracks,
All the way down to hell?
Don't say, "But, sir," just listen, there's more.
I found a bottle in his room.
He says it's his friend's.
Last week I found a pack of cigarettes in his jacket.
He swears it wasn't his.
Now my boy is lying through his teeth.
What do you got to say about that?
What? This is the library?

For God sakes, why didn't you tell me?

What's your name? Laura?

You have a nice voice, Laura.

I'm sorry I was yelling.

You sound very grown-up; sure you're not a counselor?

You don't know my boy, Eugene, Jr., do you?

Lana Novakova

I hate Laura Li
Because she is
The most popular girl in school.
She is a
Stone-hearted,
Loudmouthed,
Close-minded,
Conceited deceiver
Who thinks only of herself.
She stabs you in the back
While looking you in the face.
Once, when I had a
Problem with my parents,
She turned a deaf ear and said,
"What do I care?"
I hope she gets everything
That is coming to her.
She certainly is one of a kind,
But try telling that to my sister,
Yana.

Yana Novakova

I love Laura Li
Because she is
The most popular girl in school.
She is a
Warmhearted,
Soft-spoken,
Open-minded,
Humble achiever
Who thinks only of other people.
She touches you in the heart
While looking you in the face.
Once, when I had a
Problem with my parents,
She let me lean on her shoulder and said,
"I really care."
I hope she gets everything
That's coming to her.
She is certainly one of a kind,
But try telling that to my sister,
Lana.

Rubén Delgado

Laura Li lets me hide out in the back,
At a table deep within the reference section.
She understands I like books more than people.
She understands I like to be left alone,
And when she is not busy, she slips me
Books and magazines that illustrate
The bombers and fighters of World War II.
I draw sketches of them,
Sometimes modifying their design.
I Xerox pictures of them,
Sometimes painting them in different colors.
When I go home, I carve them in soft wood.
Finished and painted, they hang by string
From my ceiling, suspended in midflight.
I stare up at them from my bed
And wish I hadn't been born so late.
Maybe if I graduate high school,
They'll let me join the air force.
I can promise them I'd be a
Model pilot.

Sam Adamson,
President, Local Chapter,
American Legion

Yes, she wrote a beautiful essay,

A prize-winning essay,

On Chinese immigration to the United States.

Her research was impeccable,

Her conclusions, brilliant.

She explained elegantly how

America still keeps its promise

By affording newcomers ample opportunity

To share the fruits of its bounty,

Economic and political,

Opening its arms to the "huddled masses."

But unfortunately

We cannot award the prize to Ms. Li.

She is not a U.S. citizen and,

As our rules clearly stipulate,

Essay winners must be Americans.

We wish Ms. Li success

In her future educational endeavors,

And we will continue to encourage her

In whatever way we can.

After all, America is still

The land of golden opportunity.

<u>OVER</u>
DUE

<u>shelf</u>

The book is on the high

Love Letter #2

Laura Li,

There is a section of the library,

A small one,

Where all the poetry books are kept.

Nobody can find it.

Hardly anybody has used it.

Few people have disturbed the dust.

In a world where sex substitutes for love,

One date means a relationship,

And anonymous people

Declare their anonymous passion

Behind the minimask of the microchip,

True love fights to be seen and heard.

I will not buy you a Hallmark card.

I will not prove my love with a pound of stale chocolate.

I will not tell you of my love only on Valentine's Day.

I will happily return to

That forgotten section of the library

And check out the words of the old masters,

Who knew, without benefit of e-mail,
That their written words of joy and sorrow
Possessed the permanent signature of truth.

Love,
A.F.

Laura Li

(the dream)

The Roman galley
Slips out of its moorings
And plies the waters of my soul.
The captain, his eyes gray stone cold,
Looks over a black sea.
We are headed for China, I think,
Where children starve and the earth shakes.
The skeletal crew watches over
The prisoners lashed to their oars.
The oar mistress signals to the drummer,
Who pounds out the beat on the eardrum in my head.
I look at the twelve rows of prisoners, two abreast.
I look at my partner; she looks exactly like me.
"Would you like the window or the aisle seat?" she asks.
"It does not matter," I say.
I am chained forever, my arms aching,
Unable to find a safe harbor to call my own.

Carl Snider

(after "Richard Cory," by Edwin Arlington Robinson)

Whenever Ms. Laura Li walks on by,
We people in the hallways look at her:
She is a foxy chick from sole to crown,
Clean-favored, but sexy, most would concur.

And she is always quietly arrayed,
And she is always human when she talks;
But still she flutters pulses when she says,
"Good morning," and she glitters when she walks.

And she is cool—yes, cooler than a queen,
And admirably schooled in every grace:
In fine, we think that she is everything
To make us wish that we could kiss her face.

So on we work and wait for the bell,
And go without lunch and rag each other,
And Ms. Laura Li, every springtime night,
Goes home, alone, to an unseen mother.

PUBLIC ADDRESS ANNOUNCEMENT

We interrupt your
classes for a brief word
about the prom.

Myles Klutter

Laura Li,

You doin' anything Friday night,

The Friday night of the prom?

I thought if you weren't busy

I could pick you up in the limo around seven,

Me, in my rented tux, you, in your long black gown,

And we could head on over to the Plaza Terrace.

When we'd get to the prom,

I'd help you out of the limo

As all my friends would look at us,

And then at you again.

I'd have a smile on my face, ear to ear,

As I'd pin a beautiful corsage on your dress.

To tell you the truth, you don't know me very well.

I sit behind you in fifth-period history,

But we could get to know each other

Out on the dance floor, with the lights low,

Maybe even be named King and Queen of the prom.

All my friends would notice me then.

Laura Li, I could show you a good time,

That is, if you're not too busy Friday night

And my friends don't want to go someplace else.

Ernesto Rojas

Pam grows older
On my shoulder.
Mary ain't gone
From my right arm.
Jess on my wrist
Cannot be dissed.
Jen on my chest
Gives me no rest.
Tattoo, Tattoo,
What should I do?
Get a panther?
Not the anther.
Get a red rose?
Hard to dispose.
Get a smooth skull?
Oh, God, so dull.
A butterfly?
Not for this guy.
Laura, Laura,
I adore her.
Can't ignore her—but,
No room for her.

Arthur Feldman

Doing math sets in the library sucks.

I keep thinking about my social life instead.

It sucks, too.

Like this math example I'm working on,

It doesn't add up.

There is no solution to my problem.

Looking at you, Laura, I wish for a fraction of your
     attention.

Is there any chance that our lives can intersect?

I'd like to tell you more graphically of my love,

Show you some proof of my good intentions.

Maybe you can tutor me,

Explain the mysteries of algebra,

While I try to calculate the distance between us.

Maybe we can do homework together.

You doing the math, of course, while

I study the biological forces of nature.

Alejandro Felix

If I were good in English,
I'd compose graceful sonnets for you.
If I were good in French,
I'd whisper romantic words of love.
If I were good in math,
I'd figure out how to inscribe you into my circle.
And if I were good in gym,
I'd run a marathon to get close to you.
But the most important subject is chemistry,
The chemistry that quickly produces
Boiling, bubbling reactions, hot to the touch.
When you meet someone, see her face,
You know in five seconds
Whether there will be a chemical bonding.
When I met you for the first time,
When I saw your face for the first time,
All academic thoughts escaped me, but one.
I could only think of the chemistry between us,
The mixing of our essential elements,
Resulting in a nuclear explosion of love.

Laura Li

Sometimes when my mother is sewing,
We look in the mirror together,
As she fixes the hem of my skirt.
It is then we are the closest.
I try to ask her about boys,
But she won't discuss the subject.
All boys of any race or nationality are off-limits,
    she says.
If one is foolish enough to call my house,
To ask questions about homework or a test,
My mother listens in on the extension,
Making sure no verbal indiscretions have been
    committed.
The only place during the day I can talk with boys
Is here in the library, where, between words like
"This book is overdue" and "The machine is out of
    order,"
I can flirt outrageously.
The only place during the night I can dance with boys
Is in the clubs, where between songs like
"Party All Night" and "I Wanna Do It All the Time,"
I can move fast, I can move slow.

What she doesn't know would hurt her.

My mother and I look in the mirror together.

It's a pity we see two different images.

Becca Cavallero

Laura Li,
Don't tell anyone you've seen me, okay?
I just want to sit in the corner and cry.
If someone sees me sniffling,
Just tell them I'm reading a sad story.
My own.
Seven-Eleven was a constant reminder
Of the nights I stood behind the counter,
Serving greasy franks to greasy kids,
Who also tried to buy cigarettes,
Even though they were way underage.
I wanted my prom dress,
Black and lustrous,
And when I was finally able to buy it,
Tony came by and told me
He wasn't taking me to no stupid prom.
I'd like to take a beer bottle
And smash it over his head.
And I might just do that,
Right after I finish crying.
Laura Li, tell me,
Why are boys such assholes?

Tyesha Hicks

Girl, that was you, wasn't it?
That was you at the club,
Shakin' your booty so bad
It made grown men cry.
First, I says to myself it ain't you.
You're too high-and-mighty to get down.
You're too clean to get dirty.
You're too cool to be so hot.
But it was you, wasn't it?
No, I ain't playin'.
I ain't talkin' trash.
Even though it was dark,
With all kinds of colors flashin',
I know white when I see white.
And girl, there was a whole lotta white I seen.
What was you wearin'?
There was more flesh on you than fabric.
You callin' me a liar? I'll smack you.
Wish I had a camera to prove it,
'Cause, girlfriend, you was definitely
Overexposed.

Library Fun III

What?
You haven't returned your library books?
Call the Hostage Negotiating Team and
We will arrange for the return
Of these imprisoned volumes.
Bring them in at once, or
Your library pass will be discarded.
Your English teacher will render you déclassé.
But not to worry—
The security guard finds you disarming.
The physics teacher thinks you're delightful.
The creative-writing teacher won't denounce you.
The music teacher won't abandon you.
The math teacher won't disfigure you.
And the gym teacher won't disbar you.
But remember, the Library Police
Might still come to your house.
They consider you a felon,
And if the books are not returned real soon,
You will be booked on all outstanding charges.

Girard Patterson,
Custodian

You mind if I get this basket, miss?
You just go on givin' out books.
Don't mind me, I'll be outta your way in a second.
Kids today don't know how good they got it—
Free books, free lunch, free learnin'.
All they got to worry about is
Passin' a few classes.
They don't gotta worry 'bout
No rent, no groceries, no doctor bills,
Like I gotta do—little one's been sick.
What's your name?
Laura Li? That's a pretty name.
You make sure you enjoy high school,
Every day of it.
Wish I knew then what I know now.
Hey, I'm not complainin', mind you.
I love my kid, I do,
But sometimes I just feel
Like it's hard to breathe.
Know what I'm sayin?
Hey, what am I doin', bendin' your ear like this?

I don't know what it is,
But you seem to hear with your eyes.
I'll get the other basket from the back.

Laura Li

In the language of mother and daughter
We are almost mute, substituting
Weariness for words,
Caution for conversation.
We give each other space—
Plenty of it—
As we sit, alone and silent,
In different rooms.
Words, like trial balloons,
Are occasionally tossed into the air—
"Do you want some tea?"
"Are you studying for your midterms?"
"Do you wish me to cook supper?"—
Only to be deflated by one-word replies:
"No," "Yes," "Maybe."
The Great Wall of China
Does not lie far to the east,
But stands instead at the gateway
Between the computer screen in my room
And the television set in hers.

Arthur Feldman

Don't get me wrong:
I love school—
For hanging out,
For meeting girls,
For going to *some* classes.
I don't let school interfere
With my education, let alone my life.
School comes at an awkward time—daytime,
When there is so much better stuff to do.
I'd like to work on my Harley,
Installing new shocks on
The old bike I picked up from this guy's ad.
I'd like to ask Laura Li if she would ride with me.
What a thrill it would be,
Her arms around my waist
As we zip down the highway.
I wonder how I'm going to sit in my classroom
When all I want to do is run my bike,
With Laura Li pressing against me,
And the sound of her voice in my ear.

Alejandro Felix

Don't get me wrong,
I love school—
For learning new stuff,
For getting high grades,
For preparing myself for college.
I don't let my life interfere
With school, let alone my education.
School comes at exactly the right time—daytime,
When there is nothing better to do.
I'd like to work on my project,
"The Age of Pericles,"
The topic I selected from my teacher's list.
I'd like to ask Laura Li if she would help me.
What a thrill it would be,
Her hands touching the same keyboard as mine,
As we zip down the information highway.
I wonder how I'm going to sit in my classroom
When all I want to do is finish my research,
With Laura Li pressing against me,
The sound of her voice in my ear.

Arthur Feldman

Birds preen,
Birds strut,
Birds follow other birds
To the watering hole,
Fluffing their fine feathers
To work their way higher
In the pecking order of the flock.
It's just like the prom.
Sheep stare,
Sheep stroll,
Sheep follow other sheep
To the watering hole,
Bleating to their companions
To work their way higher
To be head of the flock.
It's just like the prom.
Two by two they come,
Flailing their limbs wildly on the floor,
Obeying some ancient instinct,
Following some ancient ritual,
To rise to the position of
King and Queen of the herd.

Baa-baa-baa.

Mom, can I have some money?

I'd like to ask this girl to the prom.

Amy Yau

My nose is too long,
My head's so small,
My arms are too short,
I'm not very tall.
My chest is too flat,
My hair is a mess,
How someone could like me,
Is anyone's guess.
The best years are now,
Or so I've been told,
But these years are painful,
I need to grow old.
My parents don't love me,
I feel quite alone,
I hate everybody,
Myself, to the bone.
Laura, Laura,
There's nothing to do,
My plight is hopeless.
Can I trade places with you?

Laura Li

The   Metronome
Of   My
Life   Beats
Without   Variation.
School,   Library,
Study,   Practice
Tick   Before
My   Eyes
As   I
Diligently   Practice
My   Scales.
What   Is
The   Key
Of   Me?
I'd   Like
To   Throw
My   Metronome
Out   The   Window,
And   Dance,
Dance   All
Night   Long.

Laura Li

Look, Shirley, you may be my friend,
But it's none of your business, got that?
If I want to smoke,
None of your public-service announcements
Is going to make me stop.
Don't tell me about
My lower life expectancy,
My blackened lungs,
My parents' horror at finding out.
None of that bothers me.
(Okay, maybe the part about my parents does.)
But I never light up around them and
I always carry Tic Tacs in my pocket.
My parents don't care what I do,
As long as I get good grades
And take care of my older brother, Jimmy.
I smoke nearly every chance I get—
In the girls' bathroom, the stairwells,
Even in the back room of the library
When Ms. Binder steps out.
Nobody thinks I ever do anything wrong,
Part of the image, part of the stereotype.

Let them go on believing I'm perfect.

People see who or what they want anyway.

Shirley, you got a cigarette on you?

Laura Li

I have no reservations about
Slipping out of my house
At midnight on a Saturday night
When my parents and Jimmy are fast asleep.
I have no reservations about
Meeting my club friends on the corner
And tearing down the road
To the hottest spot around.
I have no reservations about
Flirting with the bouncer so he lets me in,
Flirting with the bartender so he gives me drinks,
Flirting with the men who want to dance with me.
Let the night cover my sins.
Let the music drown out my conscience,
And in the morning,
Though I'll be hungover,
I'll have no reservations about
What I did after dark,
No reservations at all.

Eddie DeLoria,
Bartender

Hey, cutie,

Would you like to sit up here at the bar?

You want a drink?

Naah, you don't have to show me I.D.

You look old enough.

You certainly look good enough.

Tell you a secret, China doll.

You're good for business sitting up here.

Guys see you and they'll run up,

Ordering more than they can afford,

Just to impress the hell out of you.

And as long as I'm dispensing drinks here,

Let me dispense a little advice to you, doll.

The guys who are looking into your eyes

Are thinking a good deal lower.

The more charming they try to be,

The more desperate they are to score.

So, cutie, you be careful out there. . . .

But don't worry, I'm here if you need me.

You want another drink?

Tyesha Hicks

So I'm at the club,
Dancin' with my honey,
Vertically now,
Horizontally maybe later,
When he looks over my shoulder and says low,
Like I don't know what he's sayin',
"Check out that Asian thing over there.
She pure vanilla."
I spin him around and
See Laura Li starin' at my man.
"What you lookin' at?" I says.
She lowers her eyes.
"What you lookin' at?" I says, louder.
"What you makin' a scene fo'?" my honey says.
That ain't right—he stickin' up
For that white bitch, so I says,
"You be wantin' vanilla? Go right ahead,
'Cause you certainly ain't gettin' no chocolate."
"I'm just lookin', that's all."
"Lookin' is like wantin'," I says,
Turnin' round, not before sayin',

"You can play with her,
Or you can play with your own fat-assed self.
I'm goin' home."

"Doc"

We got red ones,
We got blue ones,
We got sales on
Tried and true ones.
We give credit,
We don't charge tax,
We take plastic,
We take your fax.
Trust me, baby,
I ain't the cops,
Look for me
When the music stops.
The free samples
I will supply,
They're guaranteed
To get you high.
I'll give you one,
It's your freebie,
I'm quite sure you'll
Come to see me.
Catch you later,

I'll be around,
At the club scene,
Uptown and down.

Love Letter #3

Laura Li,

When is your birthday?

Only once a year?

I'm afraid that's not good enough.

Because the day of your birth,

Whether it comes

In summer's heat or winter's cold,

Must be celebrated

By me,

Every day of the year.

Break out the balloons,

Break out the candles,

Break out the musicians

Who can play the song in my heart.

I need to celebrate

The beauty of your face,

The beauty of your soul,

The beauty of the love I feel for you.

I need to bring you presents,

Big and small, each and every morning,

To show you the mistake

The calendars make

When they say
Birthdays come only once a year.

Love,

A.F.

Alejandro Felix

Longing glances
Cut short before they are noticed,
Love letters written,
But torn up before they are sent,
Sentences begun, but not finished.
I have failed the audition to sing of my love.
When it comes to speaking to Laura Li,
The leading lady of my daytime and nighttime dreams,
I stand dazed and mute at the front desk
Where we both work.
All my rehearsed lines sound phony.
All my favorite jokes fall flat.
I want to shout out my lines to the mezzanine:
Laura Li, I love you!
What comes out in a stage whisper is,
Laura Li, do you see the stamp pad?
I want to roar out my lines to the back balcony:
Laura Li, will you marry me?
What comes out in a stage whisper is,
Laura Li, did you see the reserved book list?
But now, before anyone else gets the part,
I must command the stage and say,

While the spotlight of her smile shines on me:
"Laura Li, will you go to the prom with me?"

Arthur Feldman

"The Tortoise and the Hare"—
Remember that one?
Slow but steady wins the race.
That's a laugh.
When I finally got up the nerve
To ask Laura Li to the prom,
She lowered her eyes demurely and said,
"Alejandro just asked me,
But you're so sweet to think of me."
The tortoise becomes roadkill
As the hare runs him over
And captures the prize.
I have a few words for the tortoises of the world:
Arise, you reptiles.
You have nothing to lose but your shells.
Cast off your coverings
So people can see who you are inside.
Love is for the swiftest,
For those who will run up the beach.
It is not meant for tortoises,
Who wallow in the sand,
Afraid to stick their necks out.

Oi Pin Li

My darling daughter,
So you wish to attend the prom this year.
Why bother to ask me?
My darling daughter, I am not a fool.
Do you not think you go out enough at night?
Do you think I have not seen you in clothes
That only a lowly prostitute would wear?
Hush, I have not spoken to you about this
Because I have been overwhelmed by shame.
I have spared your father this news
Because he would send you far, far away.
You have brought dishonor to both of us.
You have laughed at our sacrifices for you.
All we asked is that you get an education
And take care of your unfortunate brother.
But this was too much of a burden for you.
We will not talk any more of this behavior.
But you are to be punished, my darling daughter.
No, you may not go out for this prom,
Or for any other social occasion.
And please bring me your father's
Old, brown leather strap,
The one that hangs in the back of his closet.

Oi Pin Li

One child, one child . . .
Before I was pregnant, the government said
Only one child was allowed in a family.
This did not bother me,
For I knew my son would grow up strong and healthy.
But when he came to resemble the bent branch of a tree,
I asked the government for one more child, one more
    child.
After many petitions and interviews I was granted my
    wish.
I was not too disappointed when my second child, second
    child
Was a girl, who flowered in the morning sun.
My husband, wanting freedom,
Secured our passage to America, the land of many
    children.
But now I am in distress more and more about
My second child, second child.
I do not like the way she talks—too American.
I do not like the way she dresses—too American.
I do not like the way she eats—too American.
She is not the Chinese child I wanted—too American.

All I have left, however ill, however bent,
Is my one Chinese child.
One child, one child . . .

PUBLIC ADDRESS ANNOUNCEMENT

The library is now closed.

Alejandro Felix

It's my nose, right?
You don't like my nose.
It's my hair, right?
You don't like my hair.
I know it can't be because I'm Hispanic.
You're not a prejudiced kind of person, Laura.
Give me one good reason why
You can't go to the prom with me.
I'll give you several why you should.
I'm handsome, I'm fun,
And, most important of all,
I love you.
I have always loved you.
I loved you even before we met.
My grandmother says there is one person
In the world you are fated to love,
And we spend our lives searching for that person.
With you, I told her my search was over.
With you, I told her my life begins.
Do you want to break my grandmother's heart—
And mine?
Why can't you go to the prom with me?
What do you mean you can't tell me why?

Sarah Binder,
Librarian

Laura Li?

Are you all right?

Are you sure?

It's just that lately you seem—

Well—down.

Am I working you too hard?

Is school working you too hard?

Is everything okay at home?

Are you sure?

Forgive me, I don't mean to pry,

But it comes with being a parent.

We nag, we scold, we criticize—

Anything to enter our children's world,

But they erect tall fences

Of silence, sarcasm, and flight

To keep us at arm's length.

I hope there is no wall between us.

You know you can talk to me about anything.

Is everything okay?

Are you sure?

I wouldn't want to lose my best assistant.

Shirley Eng

Laura Li?
Are you all right?
Are you sure?
It's just that lately you seem—
Well—down.
Forgive me, I don't mean to pry,
But I don't see you in class all the time.
Are you cutting?
I don't see you smiling in the library.
Is she giving you too much work?
I don't see you socializing in the hallways.
Are things all right at home?
You usually listen to everyone else
With compassion and charity.
Now I begin to wonder,
Who listens to you?
Where do you go for comfort?
I had thought one time
That the only thing I ever wanted
Was to trade places with you.
I don't think I would wish for that now.
Is everything okay?

Are you sure?

I wouldn't want to lose a friend.

We are friends, aren't we?

Laura Li

Daddy, where are you?

Away again on some trip?

Oh, I do not blame you.

I know you must make a living for our family.

I know you must provide for my brother, Jimmy.

I realize you are much too busy

To take me to beautiful parks,

To take me dancing,

To take me to foreign places,

Where we can sit at an outdoor café

And watch the people passing by.

I must remember that you are on a tight schedule,

With difficult clients and time-consuming conferences.

But I just want to say one more thing.

It won't take too long or interrupt your schedule.

Oh, Daddy, you could have saved me,

From her,

From myself,

If you could have saved

A little time for me.

Laura Li

There is no room to dance.
There is no room to spin.
The bright strobe lights at night
Cannot illuminate the grays of my days.
The pressure to perform
Adds so much weight to my feet
That I am unable to leap into my own life.
My dance instructor
Choreographs my steps so precisely,
I don't have the freedom
To figure out the steps
I must take for myself.
It is time, perhaps,
To look upward,
To dance without fear,
To dance without stopping
At the bar of heaven's gate.

Luís Salazar
Nelson Rubildo

"You smell that?"

"Can't smell a thing. Allergies."

"I swear I smell something."

"The cafeteria."

"Ain't that bad."

"The chem lab, then."

"No, that's way over on the other side."

"Stink bomb, maybe."

"No, it's comin' from the library."

"Cool."

"Look, look inside the door window."

"I don't see nothin'."

"There, in the corner, flames!"

"The door is locked."

"Go find the security guard."

"Anybody in there?"

"How the hell should I know?"

"Don't Laura Li work there?"

"Who's that?"

"Only the hottest girl in the world."

"If she's in there, she's toast. I'm getting help."

"Hope nothin' happened to her."

On Patrol

Copy that, we're on it.

Be there in five minutes.

Something's up at the high school, Bill.

Isn't clear what.

Boy, that school can't catch a break.

While back, a teacher gets shot,

Then another teacher goes berserko

And takes a class hostage,

And then that trouble, you remember?

First with the basketball team,

And then when those kids

Went on a trip upstate.

What's your guess this time?

Probably nothing, you think? Hope so.

But I tell ya, it's a lot harder

Goin' to school these days,

More stuff to deal with.

It's a lot harder stayin' alive.

I went to Tower.

I don't remember things bein' so rough.

We got an update:

Fire engines en route.

Step on it.

Jessica Phillips
Lisa Morris

"You hear that?"	Gong!
"Fire alarm, it sounds like."	Gong!
"A false alarm?"	Gong!
"Yeah, probably."	Gong!
"What if it's real?"	Gong!
"What do I care?"	Gong!
"What if the school's really on fire?"	Gong!
"Cool."	Gong!
"What if there is a panic and a riot and—"	Gong!
"That's cool, too."	Gong!
"And everybody gets burnt to a crisp."	Gong!
"Wouldn't have to take my math test then."	Gong!
"Wouldn't have to take any test at all."	Gong!
"Couldn't care less."	Gong!
"Maybe it's just a fire drill."	Gong!
"How dull."	Gong!
"You got a cigarette?"	Gong!
"You got a light?"	Gong!
"Had my lighter a second ago. You seen it?"	Gong!
"Didn't you have it in the library last period?"	Gong!

Dave "Slim" Conifer

Fire drill?
Leave me alone, man.
I'm restin' my head.
Went to bed at three in the A.M.
Just chillin'.
Went to the pool hall.
Nothin' happenin' there
'Cept this fight that almost broke out
Between this Jewish guy and some Latino dude.
People got in between 'em, broke it up
Before anythin' interestin' went down.
It was over this Asian girl,
This drop-dead-gorgeous China doll.
She was there, doin' nothin',
(Wish I could do her.)
Not even watchin' the two guys argue over her.
Fire drill?
Hey, clue me in later, man.

Ray Montag,
Firefighter

Engine number two, do you read me?

This is Montag,

On floor three

In the library.

Portable's not going to do it.

Charge the line!

Charge the line!

We need water now.

Flames have consumed

About a quarter of the room.

Extensive smoke.

Fire limited to the library.

Repeat: Fire limited to the library.

Get some more lines and men up here pronto.

We don't want this sucker to spread.

Checking to see if everyone's out.

What the . . .

Hold it a second.

Lieutenant, Lieutenant,

There's a body here,

A body behind the desk.

Attempting CPR.
Get the hell up here,
FAST!

Lt. Terrell Nickens,
Fire Department

Yes, the fire is under control now.

Yes, it could have been worse.

Yes, my men acted with skill and dispatch.

You'll have to excuse me now, I have to go.

Any more questions, ask my battalion chief.

Yes, we were prompt.

Yes, we were brave.

Yes, we saved what we could.

You'll have to excuse me now, I have to go.

Any more questions, ask my battalion chief.

I'm not telling you about what?

The body?

How the hell did you find out about that?

What do you want me to say?

That we found a body

Of a seventeen-year-old Asian female?

That she apparently died of smoke inhalation?

You say it.

I can't.

Jessica Phillips
Lisa Morris

"You hear that?"

"It's the all-clear bell."

"You goin' back to class?"

"What for? They ain't teachin' nothin'."

"Whaddya feel like doin'?"

"Your choice, I don't care."

"How come you in such a good mood?"

"Keep a secret?"

"Sure."

"My man, Tommy, got only two years."

"That makes you happy, girl?"

"Hell, yeah, he coulda got fifteen."

"That woulda been one long, long engagement."

"I swear when he gets out we're gonna do everything."

"He'll be horny as hell, that's for sure."

"Sex ain't everythin'."

"Sure it is. I see you scopin' those firemen."

"I'm just lookin', I ain't buyin'."

"What a cheap fire."

"Ain't nothin' got burned, just the library, I hear."

"No big loss. You ready to split?"

Sarah Binder,
Librarian

No, I am not all right.

How do you expect me to be?

My library's ruined, there's smoke everywhere.

Don't tell me to calm down, young man.

You have no right to tell me to calm down.

Is everybody all right?

Where's Laura Li, my assistant?

No, I didn't hear what the fire lieutenant said.

I told you already.

I had to go down to the main office.

There were no students inside.

I told Laura to keep the door locked.

There was nobody inside.

Alejandro didn't come in today.

He's my other monitor.

They both check out books for me.

No, I don't know where he is.

I don't know where Laura is either.

What did the fire lieutenant say?

Shirley Eng

Yes, I know Laura, she's in two of my classes.
You don't have to show me her picture.
Yes, we are friends, sort of.
Not that she's my best friend or anything like that.
I call her a "too" girl, you know—
Too smart, too pretty,
Too popular, too perfect—
Picture perfect, you might say.
Yet, I am content to stand
In the shade of her flowering tree.
I am content to listen
As she talks to everyone with ease.
I am content to hang around
Just outside her inner circle.
I don't know that much about her, really.
She pretty much keeps to herself.
But I always have the feeling
She has a lot going on inside of her.
Take it from me,
That charming, pretty picture you have there.
The one of her standing
In front of the tree, arms outstretched,

Isn't all it's cracked up to be.

Detective, why are you asking me all these questions?

Did something happen to her?

Dr. Vernon Stoker,
Medical Examiner

Smoke inhalation?
The fire itself was a smoke screen,
If you'll forgive the pun.
For what? For suicide, that's what.
Someone's blowin' smoke rings
Right past you, detective.
Yes, there was evidence
Of smoke in her lungs,
But flames didn't kill this poor girl.
She took her own life.
She took pills—
Blue ones, red ones,
The kill-you-dead ones.
Sure, I'm sure.
That's what they pay me for.
Although they don't pay me enough
To do this kind of sad work.
An accident? Hardly.
She set the fire by herself—on purpose.
I guess she wanted it to look like an accident.
Oh, one more thing to make this worse:

This young lady, this beautiful young lady,
Had a series of healed bruises
On her upper thighs and back.
She was a victim long before today.

Lyle Potash

Laura Li?

No, I don't know her, man.

But I'll tell you something.

You want the perfect girlfriend?

Forget about the cheerleader;

She's too busy goin' to practice.

Forget about the class president;

She's too busy goin' to meetings.

Forget about the girls' softball captain;

She's too busy goin' to games.

Forget about them all, friend.

Unless, of course, they're from the Far East.

Get yourself an Asian chick, man.

They know how to make a man happy.

They're smart, but not too smart.

They're sexy, but not too sexy.

They're slim, but not too slim.

Where'd I learn all about 'em?

In the movies, of course.

Where else?

Hey, man, why are you asking me all these
        questions?

Did something exciting happen in this boring
   school?

Darlene Trasher

Alejandro Felix?

No, I don't know him, man.

But I'll tell you something.

You want the perfect boyfriend?

Forget about the quarterback;

He's too busy goin' to practice.

Forget about the class vice-president;

He's too busy goin' to meetings.

Forget about the basketball captain;

He's too busy goin' to games.

Forget about them all, friend.

Unless, of course, they're from south of the border.

Get yourself a hot Latin lover, girl.

They know how to make a woman happy.

They're smart, but not too smart.

They're sexy, God how they're sexy.

They're slim, but not skin and bones.

Where'd I learn about 'em?

In the movies, of course.

Where else?

Hey, man, why are you asking me all these
    questions?
Did something exciting happen in this boring
    school?

Tyesha Hicks

Laura Li?
Of course I know her.
Everyone thinks she is such a lady,
So perfect, so polite.
My ass.
We used to be so tight;
We used to hang together, that is
Until she stole my boyfriend,
Right from under me . . . literally.
Believe me, she knew what's up,
If you catch my meaning.
But that wasn't all.
This one time we was smokin'
In the girls' bathroom and
Just as the security guard came in,
She slipped the cigarettes into my book bag.
They believed her, of course,
Because she was white,
Or maybe off-white.
Me? Not a chance.
My mother had to come up to school.
I've crossed Laura Li off my list.

Whaddya mean, do I ever do drugs?
Just because I'm black,
You think I done somethin'?

Alejandro Felix

Even if the library were open,
I couldn't bear to walk in it.
Even if all the students were inside
And Ms. Binder were at the front desk,
I couldn't take a step inside.
Without you,
The library is just, well,
Books.
And all the books in the world
Cannot contain the words
To ease the pain in my heart.
I wonder what would have happened
Had you said, "I'll go to the prom with you,"
Had you said, "I'll be your girlfriend,"
Had you said, "I'll marry you."
I have heard many wild stories about you.
I believe none of them and rely instead
On what I know and what I feel.
You made me feel alive,
You made me feel hungry,
You made me feel the music of laughter,
The lyric of conversation.

Our hearts faced each other on opposite pages.
Our feelings ran along the same lines of the same
    book.
I'm leaving this corsage at the library door.
It would have looked lovely on your prom dress.

Louis Sammler,
Principal

I have her student profile right here, detective.

It's really confidential,

But under the circumstances . . .

She was a most wonderful young lady,

Perfect in every way.

Everybody loved her.

As you know,

She worked in the library,

Tutored in our homework center,

Sang in the school chorus.

All her teachers loved her.

Look at these recommendations.

Look at her I.Q. score.

As you can see,

She had a 94 average,

Reached 1480 on her SATs.

Scored 4 on each one of her last two A.P. exams.

Numbers don't lie, sir.

She was perfect in every way.

Just ask the people who knew her.

Epilogue

Oi Pin Li

My little plant,
My darling, my precious flower,
Please forgive me.
I did not water you properly.
I did not turn your face toward the sun.
I kept you in the hothouse far too long,
To grow beautiful and elegant for my pleasure only.
Please forgive me.
I raised you in the soil of my tradition,
How I was raised, how I was nurtured.
Transplanted, you forgot your roots
And grew wild in new ground.
Now I am going back,
Back to the barren garden in the old country,
Where I must stand alone,
Among the weeds,
Among the stunted growths,
Where there is no forgiveness in nature.

Charles Li

Yes, that is my daughter's picture

Hanging on the wall.

Beautiful, isn't she?

Yes, much younger, ten years of age, I believe.

I have the same picture, only smaller,

Tucked safely like a jewel in my briefcase.

I look at it every day when I am traveling.

It was good of you to come

And pay your respects.

You are her teacher, no?

Her librarian? I don't quite understand.

But then there were many parts of my daughter's
      life

That I don't understand.

No, I don't know when we'll be going back,

But it will be sometime soon, I assure you.

We can't stay here;

I must pick up the pieces of my family

And put them together someplace else.

Yes, that is my daughter's picture,

Taken when she was much younger.

Look how beautiful she was, how innocent.

Her image will never fade from my heart.
Did you know her well?

Sarah Binder,
Librarian

I wanted to say good-bye to you, Laura,

Not at the funeral—too painful,

Not at the cemetery—too upsetting,

But here at school where I knew and loved you.

People have told me that your parents have gone back to
      China.

It's a grim tradition here at Tower

That when a student or teacher dies

We plant a tree in his or her honor,

And so on this crisp spring day,

I have lingered after the planting

Because I wanted to say good-bye to you, my child,

Because I wanted to ensure that this tree grow strong,

As you would have grown,

Had you received enough light and warmth.

Shirley Eng

There was a small obituary about you
In the newspaper the other day,
A paragraph listing the basic facts.
It did not mention how you died,
Nor the larger question of why.
It was a very discreet paragraph.
Forgive me, but how much larger, how much more joyful
The article would have been
Had it been written fifty years from now,
A page listing the fine accomplishments of a rich life.
I read the obituary over and over again,
Trying to harvest meaning from between the words,
Trying to understand why I was always envious of you,
Trying to accept the finality of your actions.
It was a very small paragraph indeed.
There should have been more to the article.
There should have been more to your life.